Nosey

"Watch closely. And try not to blink, or turn away. I do hope you haven't eaten anything recently."

Slowly, he inserted the long nail into his right nostril. When he could push it in no farther with his hand, he pounded it in with his hammer.

Scully gritted her teeth. She did not want to give Dr Blockhead the pleasure of seeing her wince. "You must be one of those rare people whose nerve endings do not feel pain," she said calmly.

Dr Blockhead smiled at her with the nail sticking out of his nose. "That's right," he said. "Just keep telling yourself that."

Other X-Files books

#1 X Marks the Spot
#2 Darkness Falls
#3 Tiger, Tiger
#4 Squeeze

Voyager

T H E ⊗ F I L E S ™

HUMBUG

A novel by Les Martin

Based on the television
series *The X-Files* created
by Chris Carter

Based on the teleplay
by Darin Morgan

HarperCollins*Publishers*

Voyager
An Imprint of HarperCollins*Publishers*
77–85 Fulham Palace Road,
Hammersmith, London W6 8JB

This paperback edition 1996
1 3 5 7 9 8 6 4 2

First published in the USA by HarperTrophy
a division of HarperCollins*Publishers* 1996

Cover photograph © Twentieth Century Fox Corporation
Cover photo by Michael Grecco

ISBN 0 00 675240 3

Set in Century

Printed and bound in Great Britain by
Caledonian International Book Manufacturing Ltd, Glasgow

To Mary Baginski,
wherever you are

Chapter ONE

It was a night straight out of a horror movie.

Black clouds billowed around a bone-white moon.

Tropical trees cast long shadows in the moonlight.

Somewhere an owl hooted, and a dog howled.

But the two boys alone in the night were not afraid. They were only seven and five. They felt safe playing in their backyard pool. They did not see the creature silently creeping toward them.

The creature had a human head and body. But it was covered with fishlike scales from head to toe, like a nightmare sea monster. The kids splashed happily as it came closer and closer.

Smoothly it slipped under the water at the deep end. Invisible as a submarine, it headed for the boys.

Then, with a hideous roar, it exploded out of the water.

The boys had no chance to escape.

They could only scream.

Then they broke into laughter.

"Daddy, cut it out!" cried the younger one.

"I knew it was you all along, Dad," the older one declared.

"You did, huh?" said Jerald Glazebrook. "Well, I've got you now!"

Glazebrook grabbed his older son, Robert, and started wrestling with him in the water.

"Oh, Dad!" shrieked Robert as they roughhoused together.

His younger brother, Lionel, got into the act. He jumped on his father's scaly back.

"Two against one. No fair!" Glazebrook said. But he kept the fun going a few minutes more.

Finally he shook the boys off.

"That's enough, kids," he said. "Your old man has had it. I got out of shape on the road. Too many shows and not enough jogging."

"I'm glad you're back home, Dad," Robert said.

"I'm glad you're home too," said Lionel.

"You see a lot of weird stuff on the road this year?" asked Robert.

"I'll have all winter to tell you about it," Glazebrook said. "But right now your mother wants you guys to get ready for bed."

Smiling, he lifted each of them out of the pool. He gave each of their rumps a mock slap and watched them run back to the house.

Then he stretched. His wet scales glistened in the moonlight.

He looked at the water. Maybe he'd do a few

laps. He'd start getting back into shape.

Glazebrook looked like a sea monster, but he didn't swim like one. He did a clumsy, splashing crawl. After ten laps he was gasping for air. He decided that was enough for tonight. Tomorrow he'd try for fifteen laps. Right now he'd just enjoy floating on his back in the cool water. Going on the road had its moments, but there was no place like home.

He thought of the van parked in his driveway. It was decorated with his show name, THE ALLIGATOR MAN, and a brightly colored painting of him in a water tank. Under the painting were the words IS HE AN ANIMAL? OR IS HE A MONSTER?

Glazebrook sighed happily. He'd be glad to give the van a rest for a while. To give himself a rest too.

Dimly he heard the dog howling in the distance. Drowsily he told himself he'd have to talk to the next-door neighbors. They simply had to stop chaining their pooch at night.

Then Glazebrook heard another sound. A splashing at the other end of the pool.

Had the kids come back? He'd have to make it clear it was their bedtime.

He lifted his head to spot them, but he saw nothing.

Then he saw ripples in the water.

Those kids, he thought. Trying to sneak up and

surprise him. Well, he'd give them a surprise when they came to the surface.

By now he could see a pale shape underwater.

It wasn't the shape of two kids. Or of one.

It was—

He didn't know what it was.

All he could make out was a kind of blob. A blob the size of a beach ball. It was heading for him faster than he could believe.

"What the devil?" he muttered, backing toward the side of the pool.

He couldn't move fast enough.

The blob slammed into him, like a cannonball hitting his stomach.

He doubled over in pain and went under.

With a desperate effort he straightened up, spitting and gasping.

The blob hit him again. He screamed. It felt as if it were breaking him in two.

He grabbed the edge of the pool. He tried to lift himself out.

"Uhhhhhhhhh!" he groaned as he was bashed from the back. Agony knifed through him. Desperately clinging to the pool's edge, he turned his head and looked down.

He saw his own blood coloring the water.

It was the last thing that Jerald Glazebrook, the Alligator Man, ever saw.

Chapter **TWO**

"You look like a fisherman who's hooked a big one," Special Agent Dana Scully told Special Agent Fox Mulder.

Mulder smiled, and Scully braced herself. She knew what kinds of things made her partner smile that way. Weird things. Things that most FBI agents wouldn't touch with a ten-foot pole.

"Take a look at this," Mulder told her.

He picked up a photo from his cluttered desk and handed it to Scully.

Scully looked at it.

Her mouth dropped open.

"Don't tell me," she said. "You've finally done it. You've gotten a shot of one of your aliens."

"No," Mulder said. "This man is human."

"My God, what happened to him?" asked Scully. "How did his head get covered with those . . . those . . . scales?"

"Nothing happened to him—except being born," Mulder said. "Here. Take a look at the rest of him."

Mulder showed Scully another photo.

This one showed the man's entire body. The scales covered him from head to toe.

"He had a rare disease from birth," Mulder explained. "It's called ichthyosis. The outside of the skin continually hardens and sheds off. Something like the bark of a tree. Fish scales, though, is what it looks like."

"Is it fatal?" asked Scully.

"Not at all," Mulder said. "It's not even painful. The suffering comes from the way other people react to it. Someone with the disease is often shunned."

"Yeah," said Scully. "People can be cruel to those who look strange."

"Beginning with the name they call them," said Mulder. *"Freaks."*

"Sticks and stones can break your bones—but names can hurt even more," Scully agreed.

"Still, this man, Jerald Glazebrook, made the best of it," said Mulder. "He picked his own name. The Alligator Man. He used it to make a good living in circuses and carnivals, and to make a good life for himself. It wasn't sticks or stones or names that killed him."

"What did?" asked Scully.

"I wish I knew," Mulder said. He showed Scully another photo. "Care to make a guess?"

Scully looked at the photo. Glazebrook lay face-down by the side of a swimming pool. Scully squinted to get a better look at the gaping wound in his lower back.

"The opening is roughly oval," Scully said. "About four inches across. I can't imagine what made a hole like that. Was the weapon found?"

"No," said Mulder.

"Any other injuries?" asked Scully.

Mulder shook his head. "The rest of him is untouched."

"A nice little puzzle," said Scully. "The local police must have their hands full."

"So do we," Mulder said. He opened up a bulging folder and took out a thick stack of photos. "Flip through these."

Scully looked at the top one. It showed a middle-aged woman with a wound in her back just like Glazebrook's. The next showed a large young man. His wound was in his midsection.

Mulder gave her the stats. "There have been forty-seven such attacks in the past twenty-eight years around the country. The first was in Oregon, the last five in Florida. The time between attacks can be as short as a day or as long as six years. The victims are all ages and races, male and female. We have no clues as to why they were killed."

"Perhaps it's some weird religious ritual," said Scully. "There are a lot of crazy cults out there."

"Negative," said Mulder. "No known cult practices this kind of slaying."

"Maybe a serial killer?" said Scully, reaching for the last photo.

"Not likely," Mulder said. "A serial killer would increase the level of violence over such a long time. These crimes show no such pattern."

Mulder put the photos back in their folder. Then he asked, "Any more thoughts, Agent Scully, about our new case?"

Scully had picked up the head shot of the Alligator Man again.

"Mulder, imagine going through your life looking like this," she said. "I wonder how he did it."

"I'm afraid it's too late to ask him," Mulder said. "But you'll still have a chance to find out."

"What do you mean?" asked Scully.

"Jerald Glazebrook had many friends," Mulder said. "We'll see them at his funeral tomorrow. We fly to Fort Lauderdale. We rent a car there to drive to Gibsonton."

"Florida?" Scully asked. "I take it Gibsonton was the victim's home."

"I think you'll find it an interesting place," said Mulder, smiling. "Full of surprises."

Chapter THREE

Mulder and Scully arrived just as the funeral service was about to begin. They found the last two empty seats in the rows of folding chairs for mourners.

The minister began to read from the Bible on a stand before him. Though he was a small man, his voice was deep and powerful:

"'The Lord is my shepherd; I shall not want. He maketh me to lie down in green pastures. He leadeth me beside the still waters. He restoreth my soul: He leadeth me in the paths of righteousness for His name's sake. Though I walk through the valley of the shadow of death—'"

Scully stifled a yawn. She had gotten up before dawn for the flight down here. Sitting in the Florida sun, she had to fight to stay awake.

Then the minister turned the page—with his bare foot. Beneath his black shawl he had no arms.

Suddenly Scully felt very wide awake.

"'I shall fear no evil: for Thou art with me; Thy rod and Thy staff, they comfort me,'" the minister read.

He looked up from the Bible and went on, "We are gathered here today to mourn the passing of Jerald Glazebrook, beloved husband, father, friend, and entertainer—"

Scully followed his eyes to where the dead man's family sat.

The two boys were dressed in dark suits. They were trying to be brave, but their lips were trembling. Their mother was dressed in black and wore a veil. The veil was not quite long enough to cover the end of her long red beard.

Scully elbowed Mulder in the ribs. "You see what I do?" she whispered.

He nodded, and together they looked around at the rest of the mourners.

Two seats down sat a woman who weighed at least four hundred pounds. She would have taken up two full chairs—except that the man beside her was thin as a skeleton.

Next to them sat a middle-aged man. As he listened to the minister's sad words, he took a long drink from a metal flask. Then he slipped the flask back into his coat pocket. Except that the coat was not really his. Scully's eyes widened when she saw that the coat belonged to a small, headless body that was growing out of the man's stomach.

"We mourn him and recall the admiration and

respect he inspired in all his fellow artists and performers," the minister continued.

Scully heard murmurs and sighs behind her. She turned her head—and saw little children filling the row of seats. But when she focused on their faces, she realized that the small people were not children at all.

A little man saw her staring. He smiled and gave her a wave of his tiny hand. She smiled weakly back.

Scully felt Mulder nudging her. She turned and followed his gaze. She looked up and up until her gaze reached the face of the giant sitting five seats away.

Scully and Mulder looked at each other.

"Feel a little out of place?" whispered Mulder.

"Do I ever," Scully whispered back. "I feel like a frea—"

Mulder put a finger to his lips.

"Don't say the word," he said. "Don't even think it. It's a word no one uses around here."

They turned their attention to the minister as he went on, "Although Jerry was a world-renowned escape artist, there is one strongbox from which none of us can escape—"

At that moment the coffin began to shake.

The minister stopped in midsentence. He stared

at the shaking coffin. Gasps and whispers ran through the audience.

"Tell me I'm not seeing this," Scully said.

"I just wish I knew *what* we were seeing," Mulder said, as the coffin shook more violently.

Someone in the back row shrieked.

A big, burly man in a sheriff's uniform marched up to the coffin. He put his massive hands on it to keep it from tipping over. Then his brow furrowed.

"Come here. Help me with this," he barked at the four pallbearers nearby.

Together they lifted the coffin and set it down a few feet away.

Now all could see what had made the coffin shake. The spot where it had been was heaving upward.

"An earthquake in Florida?" Scully wondered aloud.

"A human earthquake," said Mulder as the earth broke open and a man's head emerged.

First came a bush of wild, wiry blond hair. Then an even wilder face with the wildest eyes Scully had ever seen.

The head was followed by a naked upper body. And the rest, in black leather pants.

Finally the whole man stood before them, holding a railroad spike and a hammer.

"Let me introduce myself," he said. "Dr. Blockhead is my name. Fearful physical feats are my game."

Angry muttering greeted the intruder.

Dr. Blockhead ignored it.

"I did not know the dead man personally," he said, "so I will not give a speech about him, though I am sure he was a real nice guy and all that stuff. But I am an admirer of his work and want to pay my respects to it. Namely by ramming this spike right into my chest!"

True to his words, the wild man pressed the point of the spike against his chest and pounded it in with the hammer.

Scully started to get out of her chair. Mulder stopped her.

"Just watch," he said. "This guy is good. Real good."

Dr. Blockhead stood tall in triumph. He did not even look at the red stream trickling down his chest.

"Oh dear, I think I hit my heart," he said. "How clumsy of me."

He got no further. The sheriff grabbed him roughly by the arm.

"What do you think you're doing, hippie?" the sheriff snarled.

"Back off, Hamilton," Dr. Blockhead replied, giving the big man a violent shove.

Caught by surprise, the sheriff stumbled backward. He tripped over the coffin behind him and fell back on top of it. He lay stunned among the flowers.

Meanwhile the pallbearers rushed in to grab Dr. Blockhead. As he struggled to free himself, the mourners left their seats for a better view.

Mulder and Scully were the only ones who stayed seated.

Scully shook her head at the weirdness.

Mulder smiled.

Chapter FOUR

"I'm surprised the sheriff didn't book Dr. Blockhead for disorderly conduct," Scully said.

"I believe that you can get away with pretty strange behavior here in Gibsonton," Mulder said.

"From what we've seen so far, I think you're right," Scully said.

It was an hour after the melee at the cemetery. Jerald Glazebrook was safely in his grave at last. Scully and Mulder were waiting for the sheriff. They had set up a meeting in town at the Three Ring Diner.

The sheriff showed up five minutes after they arrived. He joined them in their booth.

"How do you like our local eating spot?" he asked.

"We haven't looked at the menu yet—but the atmosphere is interesting," Mulder said.

"Yeah," said Scully. "Makes me want to order some cotton candy."

The diner looked like a circus big top. Posters papered the walls. A trapeze hung from the ceiling. Life-size photos of performing animals and human performers seemed ready to spring into action.

"I see circuses are popular here in Gibsonton," Mulder said.

"They are," said the sheriff.

"Did Jerald Glazebrook have anything to do with the circus?" Mulder asked.

"He did," said the sheriff.

"But my files list Jerald Glazebrook's occupation as 'artist,' " said Mulder.

"Jerry was an artist—a great artist," the sheriff said. "He was the best escape artist since Houdini. He should have been a headliner in Las Vegas. He should have been a TV sensation. But his skin condition kept him stuck in sideshows. He traveled the country working in circuses and carnivals."

"I didn't think there were that many sideshows left," said Scully.

"There aren't," the sheriff said. "Just a few, barely hanging on."

"I got the impression at the cemetery that Glazebrook was not the only sideshow performer living here," Mulder said.

"Well, the sideshow folk around here are pretty much retired," said the sheriff. "Though a lot of local people do some kind of circus or carnival work."

"Why is that?" asked Scully.

The sheriff shrugged. "People in Pittsburgh work in steel mills. People here work in circuses."

"But there must be a reason for it," Scully said.

"Sure there is—if you want to go back seventy years," the sheriff said. "Performers from Barnum and Bailey's big show founded this town in the 1920s. It was a place to spend their winters. That's vacation time for circus folk. But still they like to stick together."

Scully turned to Mulder. "I think we have a lead in our investigation. Those murders took place all over the country. Someone in a touring circus or carnival could have done them. And it makes even more sense if the killer came from a sideshow. The way he or she was treated by normal people might have made the deformed person angry. Angry enough to kill."

Scully paused, then went on, "Another thing. The last five murders were all in Florida—where the sideshow performer could have retired after work dried up."

Before Mulder could say anything, the sheriff cut in. "Hold on a second, miss. I don't know much about these murders you're talking about. But I do know these sideshow performers. Around here, we call them 'very special people.' That's what they are—the nicest bunch you'll ever meet. They may look different on the outside. But it's what's inside that counts."

"That's what people say about serial killers—until they're caught," Scully argued. "Even their closest friends and family think they're completely normal. So if you call these sideshow performers normal, you also have to admit they may be capable of terrible crimes."

"Let me tell you something," the sheriff said, still hot under the collar. "Other people have a lot harder time dealing with these people's looks than the sideshow folk do themselves."

"I didn't mean to sound cruel, Sheriff," Scully said. "We're here to catch a brutal killer. It doesn't matter if he looks as odd as the Elephant Man—or as ordinary as this waitress."

The waitress had arrived at their table. She was an attractive blonde with a good figure. She smiled. "Hey, Sheriff," she said. "The usual?"

"Sounds good, Sal," the sheriff said.

Sal turned to take Scully's order.

Scully saw her other side.

Now Scully was looking at a handsome broad-shouldered man with a neat mustache and close-cropped brown hair.

"And for the lady?" Sal asked.

Scully gulped and said, "Coffee, please."

"And what's your pleasure, sir?" Sal asked Mulder, giving him a good look at "her" girlish side.

But Mulder seemed more interested in the menu.

"What is this?" he asked, pointing.

"A Barnum Burger?" asked Sal. "It's a beef patty topped with baloney."

"Not the sandwich," Mulder said. "The drawing next to it."

Scully looked at her own menu, which was decorated with sketches of famous sideshow performers. Right next to the Barnum Burger was a drawing of the oddest creature she had ever seen. Its upper part was almost human, with a shriveled head, protruding teeth, and clawed hands. Its lower part was the tail of a fish.

"Sorry, sir," said Sal. "We don't serve that. It's just part of the design."

"Too bad," Mulder said. "Then I'll just have some coffee, please."

As Sal went off to get their orders, Mulder turned to the sheriff. "The menu design is copyrighted by Hepcat Helm. Is that a local artist?"

"A bit too local," the sheriff said. "His workplace is right behind my station house."

"I'd like to talk to him," said Mulder.

Scully took another look at the drawings. It figured. Mulder and the artist could compare notes on how weird the weird could get.

Then she heard the sheriff say, "Sure, I can take you to him. But I have to warn you—the guy's a real monster."

Chapter FIVE

The sheriff first pressed the buzzer of Hepcat Helm's basement workshop. Then he knocked on the door.

"Nobody home," said Scully.

"Naw," the sheriff said. "He just can't hear us. Listen to his boom box in there."

Scully could hear the sound of heavy-metal music from inside.

The muffled beat became a blast of raw noise when the sheriff pushed open the door.

Scully and Mulder followed him into the din.

The sheriff had been right to warn them about monsters. They saw monsters everywhere they looked.

Monsters with baboon heads and forked tongues. Monsters with eyeballs dangling out of their skulls. Monsters with screaming people writhing in their jaws. Monsters of every size and shape and fearful form, luridly lifelike, painting after painting of them.

Hepcat Helm was hard at work on his latest monstrous masterpiece when the sheriff screamed his name over the blaring music.

Hepcat put down his paintbrush and snapped off his boom box.

He smiled at his visitors, baring a mouthful of yellow jagged teeth. He wasn't exactly a monster. He didn't look much like an artist, either. In his dirty Rat Fink T-shirt, greasy jeans, and black high-tops, he looked as if he should be working in an auto body shop. Scully could see construction tools lying among his art supplies and blueprints hanging among his paintings.

"Who are the rubes, Sheriff?" asked Hepcat.

"FBI Agents Scully and Mulder," said the sheriff. He turned to Scully and Mulder. "This is Hepcat Helm. He runs a carnival funhouse."

A look of pain crossed Hepcat's face. "Man, how many times do I have to tell you? Don't call it that. It's not some rinky-dink carny ride. When people go through it, they don't have fun, they have the bejesus scared out of them. It's not a funhouse. It's a Tabernacle of Terror."

The sheriff shrugged. "It's a funhouse."

"I ain't arguing no more," said Hepcat. He turned to Mulder and Scully. "The sheriff here got no artistic appreciation," he told them.

"I can see that," Mulder said soothingly. "Don't let it bother you. Artists are always misunderstood."

As Hepcat's glare softened, Mulder pulled out

the diner menu. "I was admiring this sample of your work. Very effective."

"I thought it came off pretty good," agreed Hepcat.

"I recognized most of the famous figures here," Mulder went on. "But who is this?"

"The Feejee Mermaid," Hepcat said.

"Is that what that thing is?" said the sheriff. "I wouldn't have guessed."

"That's because you don't do research like me," Hepcat said. "This is absolutely authentic. I copied it from an actual antique poster. It's the Feejee Mermaid to a T."

"What's the Feejee Mermaid?" asked Scully.

"The Feejee Mermaid is—well, the Feejee Mermaid," Hepcat said. He seemed surprised that Scully didn't recognize the name.

"It's famous in sideshow history," the sheriff explained. "A super piece of humbug that Barnum pulled off."

"Barnum billed it as a real live mermaid," Hepcat said. "But when people bought tickets, all they got to see was a monkey sewn onto the tail of a fish."

"A monkey?" said Mulder. Suddenly he looked very interested.

"A dead monkey—all dried up," said Hepcat.

"It looked so bad that Barnum had to admit it was a fake," the sheriff said.

"So that was the end of the Feejee Mermaid," said Scully. "A star one day, a has-been the next? Well, that's showbiz."

"Not at all," the sheriff said. "The Feejee Mermaid kept on being a star attraction. Barnum simply changed the way he billed it. He started calling it the greatest fake in the world."

"Barnum was a genius," said Hepcat. "He kept people guessing where the truth ended and the humbug began. When he said the Feejee Mermaid was a hoax, it made the crowds want to make sure it really was. In fact, maybe Barnum changed his story just to give the Mermaid a box-office shot in the arm. Maybe the Feejee Mermaid wasn't a fake. Maybe it was—"

Mulder finished the thought for him: "Maybe the Feejee Mermaid was real."

Scully had to smile. "Mulder, you should have been born a hundred years ago," she said. "Barnum could have used you to sell tickets. No, I take that back. He would have had you buying them."

Mulder paid no attention. He had already turned to the sheriff.

"We need to find a place to stay for the night," he said. "Any suggestions?"

"There's one place in town," the sheriff said. "The Big Top Motor Inn. It's kind of a combination motel and trailer park. A lot of traveling circus folk stay there. It's not at all fancy, though."

"That'll be fine," Mulder said. "We won't be spending much time in our rooms. We have some leads to follow."

Mulder pulled out several photos. He showed them to Scully and the sheriff.

"See these tracks?" he said. "They've been reported at several of the past crime scenes. No one was able to identify them. But one expert said they might be simian in origin."

"Simian?" said the sheriff. "That means like a monkey, right?"

"It refers to any apelike creature," Mulder said. "But in this case, quite possibly a monkey."

"You think the Feejee Mermaid is going around the country committing murders?" the sheriff said, shaking his head in disbelief. "You can't really imagine—"

"You don't know my partner, Sheriff," Scully said. "Ever heard of the statistic that made Barnum rich?"

"What one's that?" the sheriff asked.

"The one about the kind of person born every minute," said Scully.

Chapter SIX

By now Scully was not surprised by anything she saw in Gibsonton. Not even by the manager of the Big Top Motor Inn.

She barely blinked when he stood up from the registration desk to greet them.

He was three feet tall.

At his heels was his dog. It was the size of a large rat.

"Hiram B. Nutt at your service," he said in a deep voice. "I take it you two want a room. Let me suggest our honeymoon suite. Lovely, really, and quite a bargain."

"We need two rooms, near each other," Mulder said. "Ms. Scully and I are business associates."

"I believe I can fix you up," Nutt said. "We have two vacant trailers, side by side."

"That'll be fine," said Mulder. Then he looked at Nutt and asked, "Tell me, have you done much circus work in your life?"

Nutt drew himself up to his full height. "And what makes you think I've ever even gone to a circus, let alone been a slave in one?" he demanded.

"I'm sorry," said Mulder. "I know that many citizens here are former circus hands. So I thought—"

Nutt gave a loud sniff. "You thought that because I am of small stature, the only career I could have would be in the circus," he declared. "One quick look at me, and you thought you knew everything about me."

"Well, I—" Mulder started to apologize.

But Nutt was not finished. "It did not occur to you that someone of my height could have a degree in hotel management."

Nutt pointed at a framed diploma on the wall. "Or that I could have worked in the finest hotels in the country," he continued. "As a manager—not as a page boy in a childish uniform."

"Look, I didn't—" Mulder began again.

But Nutt was not ready to stop. "No. In your eyes, a diminutive person like me could not be a respectable businessman, but only a . . . a . . . clown!"

Finally Mulder managed to say, "I didn't mean any offense."

"Offended? Why should I be offended?" Nutt demanded. "It's human nature to make quick judgments of people based only on their looks. Why, I have done the same thing to you."

"Have you?" said Mulder. "And what have you concluded?"

"I have taken in your all-American face, your unsmiling expression, your boring necktie. I have decided you work for the government," Nutt said. "You are—an FBI agent."

"Am I really?" Mulder said.

"I hope you get my point," Nutt said. "I want to show how stupid it would be to look at you as a type, rather than as an individual."

"But I am an FBI agent," Mulder said, showing Nutt his badge.

There was a loud silence.

Then Nutt said, "Sign the book, please."

Mulder picked up a pen from the counter, signed the registration book, then handed the pen to Scully.

"You are also an FBI agent?" Nutt asked.

"Yes," said Scully.

"But you're a woman," Nutt said in a bewildered voice.

"Maybe you haven't noticed it, but the world is full of unusual things," Scully said, handing Nutt his pen.

Without another word, Nutt rang the service bell.

When the bellboy appeared, Scully recognized him.

She had seen him at the funeral. Or rather, she had seen *them* at the funeral. The bellboy was the middle-aged man with the headless body coming out of his midsection.

His flask was out of sight. But from the way he was walking, he looked as if he had emptied and refilled it quite a few times.

"Lanny will take your bags and show you to your rooms," Nutt said shortly.

"This way," Lanny said in a slurred voice.

He picked up their bags, straightened up, and half stumbled out the door.

Mulder and Scully walked on either side of him as he wove his way toward their trailers.

"Tell me, have you done much circus work in your life?" asked Mulder.

Scully started to apologize for Mulder's crude question. The tirade from Nutt had been enough for the day.

But before she could speak, Lanny replied with pride, "I spent most of my life on the stage. I was a headliner."

"Didn't it bother you to have people staring at you?" asked Scully.

"Best job I ever had," Lanny stated firmly. "All I had to do was stand there. Every so often I'd say, 'Ladies and gentlemen, I'd like you to meet my brother, Leonard. Excuse him—he's shy.'" As he spoke, Lanny gestured toward the small body that was joined to his.

"Your act went over big, then," Mulder said.

"Big laughs, let me tell you, big laughs," said Lanny, remembering his glory days.

"Why'd you give it up?" Mulder asked.

Lanny grimaced. "Mr. Nutt, the kindhearted manager here, convinced me to. He told me it was wrong to make my living by displaying my deformity. So I quit the circus to save my dignity. And now I carry other people's bags."

With that, he set down the luggage and mopped his face with a handkerchief.

"Those are your trailers up ahead," he said, handing Mulder the keys. He bent to pick up the bags again. But Mulder stopped him.

"Don't bother," Mulder said. "We can manage from here."

"Why, thank you," said Lanny, shaking hands with Mulder.

"Good night, sleep tight, don't let the bedbugs bite," he mumbled. "Not to say that we have bedbugs. I just meant not to, uhh, let the—"

"Feejee Mermaids bite," Mulder suggested.

"Yeah!" said Lanny. Then his brows knit. "Feejee Mermaids?"

He gave up. It was too much for him. He staggered away, flask in hand.

Mulder watched him go, then looked down at his hand.

"What's wrong?" asked Scully.

Mulder showed her a dollar bill. "Lanny slipped it into my palm as a tip," he said.

"Say, Mulder, what's all this Feejee Mermaid business?" Scully said. "You can't be serious."

"Every murder investigation needs a list of suspects, Scully," Mulder said. "We have to keep our eyes out for any unusual person or thing. We can't cross off any possibilities."

"I agree," Scully said. "But there is a problem."

"What's that?" Mulder asked.

"In this town, your list of suspects is going to read like the telephone book."

Chapter SEVEN

That night Mulder was beset by bad dreams. He tossed and turned on the lumpy bed in his trailer. Scully, in her trailer, had bad dreams also.

But Hepcat Helm had a nightmare worse than both of theirs combined.

And Hepcat was not even asleep.

Late at night was Hepcat's favorite time to work. Tonight he was in his studio putting the finishing touches on a funhouse mirror.

He stepped back to admire his handiwork. In the mirror his reflection looked like a long, horribly twisted snake.

"Perfect," he said to himself. "That'll give the customers their money's worth."

Then his eyes widened.

Beside his image in the glass was another twisted shape.

It too was long and pale, weirdly twisted.

"What the—" he muttered.

He wheeled around, angry that someone had barged into his studio.

But even the hideous image in the mirror did

not prepare him for the sight that met his eyes.

"Nooooo!" he screamed, throwing up his hands to defend himself.

His hands did no good. They could not shield him from the force that smashed into him.

Craaack!

The back of his head hit the mirror, splintering it into a thousand pieces.

Hepcat Helm's nightmare ended not with waking— but with endless sleep.

Mulder woke at dawn with his nightmare still on his mind.

He decided to go for a jog. He wanted to work up a warm sweat, not a cold one. And he wanted to clear his head.

But when he got outside, he felt as if he were back in his bad dream. Swirling mist shrouded the early morning. Nevertheless, he started running. The fog was sure to lift as the sun rose higher.

The fog was still thick when he reached a narrow bridge four miles away. Mulder paused. Should he cross or turn back?

He had run hard. He stood by the river breathing deeply. Then he saw something that made him hold his breath.

A head broke through the surface of the water.

It was the head of a bald man, with a fish wriggling in his jaws.

Mulder watched the man emerge from the river onto the bank.

His dripping body was as hairless as his head. His skin was covered with blue, red, and green tattoos.

He was a man straight out of a nightmare. And the nightmare grew worse as he squatted on the bank and began to eat the live fish.

Mulder began to tiptoe over the bridge.

The man had hearing like a cat's. Still chewing, he lifted his head at the first faint sound of Mulder's approach.

Then he was off and running. He was short and squat, but he ran like a deer.

Even fresh, Mulder couldn't have caught him. Leg-weary from his jog, he gave up after a hundred feet. Puffing, he watched the man vanish in the mist.

"Coffee," Mulder muttered to himself. "Got to have coffee. Got to wake up."

Scully was awakened that morning by a loud knocking on her door. Groaning, she sat up in bed. She waited a minute, hoping the knocking would go away. It only got louder.

She pulled on her robe and opened the door.

Lanny was standing there.

"Excuse me, ma'am," Lanny said. "But the sheriff—he wants to see you."

"Uh-huh," said Scully. Perhaps because of her dream, she was unable to take her eyes off Lanny's Siamese twin.

She knew she shouldn't stare, but the sight drew her eyes like a magnet.

It was her first chance to get a long, close look at the strange creature attached to Lanny's midsection. She saw that though it did not have a fully formed head, it did have a kind of hump rising from between its shoulders. On that hump were openings that could be eyes and ears. She could not see the rest of its body, though. It wore a jacket that matched Lanny's own, except that the sleeves were pinned to the sides. She supposed it had no arms.

She forced herself to stop staring at it and looked into Lanny's eyes. For a change, they were cold sober.

"There's been another murder," Lanny said.

Chapter **EIGHT**

An hour later Scully was kneeling beside Hepcat Helm's body. The sheriff stood nearby, watching her work. Mulder was checking out the rest of Hepcat's workshop.

Scully had a degree in medicine as well as one in science. But the wound in Hepcat's midsection puzzled her.

"It looks like the same kind of wound that killed Jerald Glazebrook," she told the sheriff. "Which means the same killer probably did it. Other than that, we're still at square one."

"I disagree," said Mulder, joining them. "We have a trail to follow now."

"What kind of trail?" asked Scully.

"A trail of blood."

"I know the corpse is covered with blood," Scully said. "But I don't see what that tells us, except that Hepcat bled to death."

Then she saw the blood-splattered drawing on the floor near Hepcat.

It was a drawing of the Feejee Mermaid.

"Is this what you mean, Mulder?" she asked

dubiously. "I think we should give that theory of yours a rest."

"The drawing is interesting," Mulder said. "But I'm talking about something else."

He indicated a track of dried blood that led from the corpse to a window at the back of the workshop.

"Take a look at the window," Mulder said.

Scully saw that the inside was covered with blood.

"So the killer pushed the window open to get out," Scully said. "What does that give us—except more of Hepcat's blood?"

"I'm not talking about *that* window," Mulder said. "Examine the small one above it. I think that's the one the killer used to get in."

Scully stood on tiptoe.

At first she saw nothing. Then she said, "That stain, on the outside of the glass. It looks like a smear of blood."

"I'd be surprised if it weren't," Mulder said. "The killer made that smear when he came in."

"But how could there be blood before the murder? That doesn't make—" Then Scully got Mulder's point.

"I see," she said. "The blood on the outside of the window didn't come from Hepcat. It came from the killer."

Mulder smiled. "We'll have to run tests on it," he said.

"We can find out the blood type at the local hospital lab," Scully said. "That'll cut down the list of suspects. But only the DNA can pinpoint the killer, and I'd have to send a blood sample up to Atlanta for that. It might not come back for weeks. The process is slow and painstaking—and they have quite a backlog."

"We might not have that long before the killer strikes again," Mulder said. "It seems he's shifting into high gear. The time between deaths is getting shorter. Something is driving him into a frenzy."

"Maybe he feels threatened because we're here," Scully suggested.

"Maybe, maybe not," Mulder said. "It's hard to know, when nothing about these crimes makes sense."

"You can say that again," the sheriff said. He had been following their conversation. "I mean, why didn't the killer come in through the open door? It's practically impossible for anyone to squeeze through that little window. The killer would have to be a cross between an acrobat and a contortionist."

"Right," said Mulder. He gave the sheriff a smile. "You could say he belonged in a circus."

"Or in a padded cell," the sheriff said.

"Let's see, whom do we know who's both talented and crazy?" mused Scully.

Her eyes met Mulder's, and he gave her a nearly invisible nod.

"Could you take the blood samples to the lab, Sheriff?" she asked. "We have to pay a call on someone."

"There is one crazy guy," Scully said to Mulder.

High above them, a man dangled upside down from a rope at the top of the flagpole. Bound in a straitjacket, he was wiggling like a fish on a line to free himself.

On the ground below him, water bubbled in a huge black pot over a small fire.

An automatic pulley was lowering the man slowly toward the boiling cauldron.

In another few minutes he would be cooked like a lobster.

He was a few feet from the boiling water when he pulled the straitjacket over his head and threw it to the ground.

Then he flipped himself upright and grabbed the rope with his hands. Holding the rope with one hand, he raised his feet and untied the rope around his ankles.

He leaped to the ground triumphantly and

pulled a stopwatch out of his pants pocket. Only then did he notice Mulder and Scully.

"No applause?" Dr. Blockhead asked. "How many people do you know who can get out of a straitjacket in under three minutes?"

"None, fortunately," Scully said.

"I see you have no artistic appreciation." Dr. Blockhead sounded annoyed.

"On the contrary," said Mulder. "We caught your act yesterday at the funeral. That was some trick with the railroad spike."

Dr. Blockhead glared at Mulder. "Dr. Blockhead does not perform so-called tricks," he declared.

"You could have fooled me," Mulder said. "In fact, you did. It just goes to show, sometimes you can't believe your own eyes."

"Well, let's see if I can make a believer of you," Dr. Blockhead said, walking to a table spread with dozens of shining metal instruments. They all looked very sharp.

"Dr. Blockhead performs many feats even more astounding than the one you saw at the cemetery," he announced. "Feats that boggle the mind. Feats that defy the most agonizing pain."

He picked up a pair of wicked-looking hat pins that were topped with metal human skulls.

He looked at them and shook his head. "Not

good enough," he said. "Not for an audience of suspicious FBI agents. I need something a bit more impressive."

He put down the pins and picked up a hammer and an extremely long nail.

"Perfecto," he said. "Watch closely. And try not to blink, or turn away. I do hope you haven't eaten anything recently."

Slowly he inserted the long nail into his right nostril. When he could push it in no farther with his hand, he pounded it in with his hammer.

Scully gritted her teeth. She did not want to give Dr. Blockhead the pleasure of seeing her wince. "You must be one of those rare people whose nerve endings do not feel pain," she said calmly.

Dr. Blockhead smiled at her with the nail sticking out of his nose.

"That's right," he said. "Just keep telling yourself that."

Still smiling, he put down the hammer and picked up a pair of pliers. He gripped the nail head with the pliers and began to yank.

"Have you ever performed this tri—I mean, stunt, on anyone else?" Mulder asked.

Dr. Blockhead paused with the nail halfway out of his nose.

"I tell my audiences that if they're stupid enough

to try this, they'll wind up with a hole where their feeble brain was. But since you guys are obviously Feds, go ahead."

"Thanks—but no thanks," Scully said.

"Wise decision," Dr. Blockhead said. "Leave this to a professional."

He fitted the pliers onto the nail head again. But before he could give them another yank, Mulder stepped forward.

"May I?" Mulder asked.

"Be my guest," Dr. Blockhead said, slapping the pliers into Mulder's palm.

Weighing the pliers in his hand, Mulder asked, "Exactly how does one become a professional block-head?"

"I had my first training when I was growing up in Yemen," Dr. Blockhead said. "After that, I traveled the world to study under the greatest masters of body control. I have been the student of yogis, fakirs, swamis, and others who know the secrets of this ancient art."

"Then I guess it's okay for me to do this," said Mulder, giving the nail a strong, sharp yank with the pliers.

The nail came free easily. Bright red blood glistened on its tip.

"Well done," said Dr. Blockhead, smiling. "I

could use you as my assistant if you'd ever like to change jobs. Of course, your partner here would be better. Audiences love a pretty girl—if she has a strong stomach."

He turned to Scully. "I'm sorry if I caused you any discomfort. But you did ask for it."

"Not to worry," Scully assured him, hoping her face had not turned green. "Actually, I'm glad you put on your little show. After that, nothing is going to bother me."

"Really?" said Dr. Blockhead. "Shall we put your statement to a little test?"

Before Scully could answer, Dr. Blockhead did just that.

Chapter NINE

I'm not seeing this, Scully tried to tell herself.

But she had to believe her own eyes.

First Dr. Blockhead went to the cauldron.

Then he gave it a sharp rap with his hammer.

A man's head broke through the surface of the bubbling water.

The head was totally bald. It was followed by a hairless body covered with tattoos as the man lifted himself out of the pot.

He stood dripping before them, wearing a loin-cloth and smiling broadly.

"Lady and gentleman—or I should say, FBI agent and FBI agent—meet Conundrum," Dr. Blockhead announced.

Scully saw Mulder's mouth drop open as if he were seeing a nightmare come to life.

Dr. Blockhead looked pleased as Punch. He did everything but take a bow. To see shock in his audience delighted him more than applause.

"What's the matter?" he asked. "Haven't you ever seen a man climb out of the water before?"

Mulder swallowed hard. "As a matter of fact, I

have," he said. "I saw him down at the river this morning. He was eating a live fish."

Now it was Dr. Blockhead's turn to be shocked. More than shocked. Angry.

Scowling, he said, "I've told him again and again never to do that. Between-shows snacks ruin his appetite."

"I could be mistaken," said Mulder. "Maybe it was a different bald-headed, jigsaw-puzzle-tattooed guy I saw."

"Does this man, this—?" Scully asked Dr. Blockhead, then paused. "What is his name again?"

Mulder supplied the answer before Dr. Blockhead could. "Conundrum."

"Does Mr. Conundrum practice body control too?" asked Scully.

"Not really," Dr. Blockhead said. "I've taught him a few simple skills, like staying submerged in boiling water. But he has a different specialty. In the language of the circus, Conundrum is a geek."

"A geek?" said Scully.

"He eats live animals," Mulder explained.

"He eats anything," said Dr. Blockhead. "Live animals. Dead animals. Rocks. Lightbulbs. Corkscrews. Battery cables. Cranberries."

"What about human flesh?" asked Scully sharply. She was not talking to Dr. Blockhead. She was questioning Conundrum himself.

44

Conundrum answered with a twisted smile. Then a crazy laugh.

"Conundrum does not answer questions," Dr. Blockhead said smugly. "He *is* a question. He is a walking riddle, a maddening mystery. When audiences see his famous Human Piranha act, they are forced to ask themselves how he can do such inhuman things—and why?"

"A good question," said Scully.

"Yeah," said Mulder. "We'll have to chew it over."

A smile spread over Dr. Blockhead's face. "But where are my manners?" he said. "What a bad host I am. Let me offer you a little refreshment."

He picked up a jar, opened it, and held it out to Scully.

"Is that what I think it is?" she asked.

"The finest assortment of living crickets money can buy," said Dr. Blockhead. "And all quite recently captured. If you don't believe me, read the expiration date on the label."

"I believe you," said Scully, still peering at the contents.

She reached in and picked out her cricket. Then she put it in her mouth and crunched down.

She smiled at Dr. Blockhead. "Thank you so much for the treat," she said.

Then she gave him a dazzling smile and walked away.

"That Scully," said Mulder, shaking his head. "She's just full of surprises."

He lifted his hand in farewell to Dr. Blockhead and Conundrum. Then hurried after Scully.

When he reached her, he said, "Remind me never to play a game of dare with you. I can see you'd stop at nothing to win."

In response, Scully reached behind Mulder's ear. With a smile, she pulled out a live cricket.

"It's an old sleight-of-hand trick my uncle once taught me," she said. "He was an amateur magician. But he still was better than those two jokers."

When Mulder didn't answer, she said, "It's all trickery, right? I mean, those things that Dr. Blockhead does to himself—they can't be real. And the so-called boiling water that Conundrum was under. There was some kind of machine to create the bubbling effect. And Mr. Conundrum had a scuba tank."

"Probably," Mulder said.

"Probably?" said Scully. "I'd say certainly."

"I know it goes against your grain to think so— but there's nothing certain in the circus, Scully," Mulder told her. "It's like an onion. You peel off layer after layer of humbug to get to the truth. And you wind up with—nothing."

"Humbug or no humbug, Hepcat Helm's bloody corpse was real enough," Scully said.

"So was the killer's blood at the crime scene," Mulder said. "And so was the blood on the nail I yanked from Blockhead's nose. And so is this—"

Mulder extended his hand and plucked a long nail out of the air—a nail with dried blood on its tip.

"Everybody's uncle is an amateur magician," he told Scully.

Chapter TEN

"Maybe this nail will nail Dr. Blockhead," said Mulder. "We'll see if the blood on it is a match for the blood on the window. I'll take it over to the lab."

"It still won't be proof positive," Scully reminded him. "Just a general blood type."

"It'll be better than what we have on him now," Mulder said. "Which is exactly nothing."

He wrapped the nail carefully in a clean handkerchief and put it in his pocket.

"Coming with me?" he asked Scully.

"You go by yourself," Scully said. "I want to do some research on my own. This circus world is pretty strange to me. I need to find out more about it. Get my bearings."

"How?" asked Mulder.

"I saw some kind of circus museum on Main Street," Scully said. "I'll start there."

"Good idea," said Mulder. "We can meet tonight back at your trailer."

Mulder took their rental car to go to the lab, and Scully headed out of the Big Top Motor Inn trailer park on foot.

As she walked along the rows of trailers, she passed an acrobatic human pyramid, one man throwing knives at another, and a crowd of tiny people who were practicing getting in and out of a very small car. Each group stopped what it was doing to watch her go by.

It was the same when she walked down Main Street. An enormous strongman carrying a mountain of groceries gawked at her. The woman behind him, carrying a shopping bag in each of her three hands, did the same. So did the man whose single leg came down from the center of his body.

So this is what it's like to look different, Scully thought. *It is not easy.*

She felt a rush of relief when she finally reached the museum. She wanted to get quickly inside and out of sight.

From the outside, the museum looked like a ramshackle country store. A big sign above the door read THE ODDITORIUM.

A collection box hung on the door. Scully read the notice on it: FREAKS FREE! OTHERS PLEASE LEAVE DONATION.

Do I qualify to get in free in Gibsonton? she wondered. To be on the safe side, she stuffed a couple of dollar bills into the box before entering.

A bell tinkled, and a tall old man in a threadbare black suit greeted her as she walked in.

"Welcome to my museum," he said. "May I answer any questions you might have?"

Scully did not ask the first question that came to her mind.

What had happened to the man's face?

Had he been born looking like that, with his features running together like melted wax? Or was it the result of a strange disease or a horrible accident?

But that's the kind of question you avoid in this town, Scully thought.

"Thank you very much," she said. "I may take you up on your offer. But first I'd like to look at some of your exhibits."

"Be my guest—and I will be your guide," the old man said.

He led her to a wall covered with large, old black-and-white photos, many of them from the turn of the century.

As Scully looked at them, the old man reeled off their names. "This is Prince Randian, the Human Torso. Here's Frank Lentini, the Man with Three Legs. This one is the Tocci Brothers, joined together and sharing just one pair of legs. And then we come to Chang and Eng, the One and Only Original Siamese Twins."

In front of the life-size photo of Chang and Eng was a table with a stack of pamphlets.

The old man handed one to Scully.

"Do read it when you have a chance," he urged her. "It is a little something that I authored."

Scully read its title: "The Fascinating True Life Story of the Original Siamese Twins."

"I'm sure that their life was quite fascinating," she said. "But tell me, was their death fascinating as well?"

"Why do you ask?" the old man said.

"I'm down here investigating the death of a—very special person," Scully said. "Anything I learn about sideshow people might help."

"Well, let me tell you that Chang and Eng's death was fascinating indeed," the old man said. "On a cold January morning in 1874, Eng woke to find that his brother had passed away during the night. A few hours later, Eng himself departed from this world."

"That's interesting," said Scully politely. But there was a puzzled note in her voice.

"I see you miss my point," the old man said. "Their deaths are not what is fascinating. It's the idea of Eng lying there alone." The old man's hand closed on Scully's shoulder, and his voice turned harsh. "You know that one half of your body is dead. And that the rest must follow. And that there is absolutely nothing you can do about it."

The man released his grip. "Fascinating indeed." said Scully. "But tell me, what was the official cause of death?"

"Chang died of a cerebral hemorrhage."

"And Eng?" Scully asked.

"Fright," the old man answered.

Scully felt a shudder run through her. She changed the subject.

"Do you have any information on blockhead or geek acts?" she asked.

"This is a historical collection of human curiosities," the old man said. "Blockheads are skilled performers."

"Like magicians?" Scully asked.

"Like sword-swallowers."

"And geeks?" asked Scully.

"Geeks are not skilled. They are not curiosities. They are merely—unpleasant. They do not even rate as high as gaffs."

"Gaffs?" said Scully.

The old man pointed to another photo.

"Another pair of Siamese twins?" said Scully. The two men were joined at the waist, sharing one pair of legs.

"You have a lot to learn, young lady," the old man said with a smile. "Take a look at their faces. Their features are distinctly different. Siamese twins are always identical. These gentlemen are phonies. They are gaffs."

Scully looked more closely at the photo, and nodded.

"I see it now," she said. "They're two guys. One has his legs wrapped around the other's waist. Their baggy pants hide it. Tell me, are such frauds common in sideshows?"

"I will only say that there are several well-known ones," the old man said.

"Like the Feejee Mermaid?" asked Scully.

The old man's only answer was a low chuckle.

"Please, I'd appreciate anything you could tell me about the Mermaid," Scully said. "It might have some bearing on the murder I'm investigating."

"If you're interested in the death of the Alligator Man, I have something you might want to read," the old man said, handing Scully another pamphlet. Below its title, "The Exotic Life of Jim-Jim, the Dog-Faced Boy," was a photo of a boy whose face was completely covered with long hair.

"What connection does this have with the Glazebrook murder?" asked Scully.

Again the old man smiled. "Perhaps something. Perhaps nothing. You will have to find out for yourself."

"Thanks—I hope," Scully said, tucking the

pamphlet into her pocket. "I really appreciate any help you can offer."

The old man looked at Scully hard. He bit his lip, as if trying to decide something. Then he leaned his melted-wax face close to hers.

"If you *really* want to understand that murder," he said quietly, "there's something you should see."

"What is it?" Scully asked.

"Come with me," the old man said.

He led Scully to a door at the rear of the museum.

"I have recently come into possession of an authentic P. T. Barnum exhibit," he told her. "I do not show this display to all visitors. It is only for those who truly want to see it, and who have enough courage to face it. Barnum called it the Great Unknown. Tell me, do you dare to risk viewing it?"

"Will it help solve the case?" asked Scully.

"You have my word," the old man said.

"Open the door," Scully said.

"First I must ask you two favors," the old man said.

"Anything. What are they?" Scully said.

"Tell no soul what you witness in there," the old man said.

"Including my partner?" asked Scully.

The old man thought a moment. "Well, perhaps just your partner. But no one else," he cautioned.

"It's a promise," Scully said. "And the second favor?"

"An additional donation of twenty dollars—to help cover what it cost me," the old man said.

Scully thrust the money into his hand.

The man pocketed the twenty, unbolted the door, and opened it.

Scully rushed through the doorway.

The moment she was inside, the door closed behind her.

She heard it being bolted on the other side.

She was locked in alone with the Great Unknown.

Chapter ELEVEN

Scully looked around her. She was locked in a small, windowless room, lit by one weak lightbulb. The walls were concrete, spiderwebbed with cracks, sweating with moisture. The air was chill and damp.

This place is like a tomb, she thought, and shivered.

There was only one object in the room, an old wooden strongbox with air holes drilled in its sides. Massive chains fastened it to the concrete floor.

Well, at least it's not a coffin, she thought. *Those air holes mean something in it is breathing.*

Scully saw that the large lock on the lid was unfastened.

I'm in luck—I guess, she thought as she squatted down and removed the lock.

She paused. She took a deep breath. She tried to relax her tense muscles. Then, slowly, carefully, she lifted the angrily creaking lid.

She was ready for anything—anything but this.

She was staring into an empty box.

At that moment a bright red neon sign lit up on the wall.

It said EXIT.

In its light Scully saw the outlines of a door.

She grimaced.

This museum had given her a real taste of the circus world, all right.

She had been humbugged.

As Mulder approached Scully's trailer that night, he stiffened.

A scurrying noise, followed by the sound of heavy breathing, was coming out from under it. Mulder froze. He didn't like carrying a gun. But he was glad to have one at a time like this.

Weapon in hand, Mulder got down on his hands and knees. He started to crawl under the trailer.

And came face-to-face with Hiram Nutt, who was crawling out.

Both of them scrambled to their feet.

"Does Agent Scully know you were under her trailer?" Mulder demanded.

"I was merely fixing her plumbing," Nutt replied.

"Uh-huh. Sure. And what else?" Mulder asked.

At that moment Scully opened her door.

"Mr. Nutt," she said. "Thanks a lot. The sink works fine now."

Nutt shot Mulder a look of triumph and strode away.

"What are you doing with your gun out, Mulder?" Scully asked.

"Just checking if it needs oiling," he said, and stuck it back into his shoulder holster. Quickly he changed the subject. "Find out anything at the museum?"

"You could say that," said Scully. She held the trailer door open for him. "So," she said, once he was inside, "tell me how the lab tests came out."

"The blood from the window matched the blood on the nail," Mulder said. "But both were O positive, the most common blood type. I also ran a background check on Dr. Blockhead. His real name is Jeffrey Swaim. He's not from Yemen, he's from Milwaukee. And he has no right to call himself a doctor of any kind."

"Any criminal record?" asked Scully.

"Nothing but a few dozen traffic violations," Mulder said. "Then, with Sheriff Hamilton's help, I ran background checks on the old sideshow performers around here. Everyone was clean."

"As a matter of fact, I ended up running a background check too," Scully said. "Just to keep my afternoon from being a total waste."

"On whom?" Mulder asked.

Scully opened a folder and started reading. "An orphan was discovered in the wild forests of Albania in 1933. He was skilled at catching his own food, but he could not speak a word, except for a few savage grunts—"

"Interesting," Mulder interrupted. "But what does this have to do with—"

"Keep listening. It gets even more interesting," Scully said, and read on. "He was brought to this country and exhibited in a locked cage. He terrified audiences with his ferocity as he devoured raw chunks of meat. He then succeeded in running away from the circus. He vanished from sight, until he reappeared in Gibsonton. Here, strange to say, he took up a career in law enforcement. He proved highly capable—and for the past four terms he has served as sheriff."

"You're telling me this is Sheriff Hamilton?" said Mulder.

"I'm telling you that before becoming Sheriff Hamilton, he was—Jim-Jim, the Dog-Faced Boy."

From her folder Scully pulled the pamphlet she had been given in the museum. Mulder stared at the photo of the boy on the cover.

"Hard to believe," he muttered.

"Believe it or not," said Scully. "Which should be the town motto."

Mulder sighed. "I suppose we have to add Sheriff Hamilton to our list."

"Just what we need—another suspect," said Scully.

"Let's pay the sheriff an after-hours visit," said Mulder. "Who knows, we might dig something up."

"I hate to think what," said Scully.

An hour later, Scully's words came back to her.

She was crouching with Mulder in the shrubbery of Sheriff Hamilton's backyard.

The sheriff, looking menacing and massive in the moonlight, was hard at work digging a hole in the yard. At last he stopped, laid aside the shovel, and mopped his brow. Then he bent and reached into the earth.

Scully gave Mulder a questioning look.

Mulder shook his head. He couldn't tell what the sheriff had pulled out of the hole either.

But there was no mistaking what the sheriff now picked up from the grass. In the moonlight a long knife glinted.

The sheriff made a cut on whatever he had unearthed. Then he rubbed it over his hands.

Finally he bent and returned it to the hole, pushing the dirt back over it.

He stood erect, stared up at the full moon, then turned and went back into his house.

"I don't want to say what I'm thinking," Scully whispered. "I mean, it's not completely scientific.

On the other hand, there have been reports over the centuries. And there's no denying it's a full moon."

"True, but we have to watch ourselves," Mulder whispered back. "Just because Sheriff Hamilton once had an excess of hair, it doesn't mean that he's a—"

"I agree," Scully said. "It wouldn't be fair to say that his affliction makes him behave abnormally. It would be like guilt based solely on skin color."

"Right," said Mulder.

"Right," said Scully.

"Still—" Mulder said.

"Still—" Scully echoed.

"Well, time to find out the truth," said Mulder. He crawled into the yard on hands and knees. Scully followed.

With his bare hands Mulder dug at the loose earth. After a minute he said, "I've got it. I just have to pull it out and—"

He got no further.

He and Scully were blinded by a high-powered flashlight.

When their vision cleared, they saw the sheriff looming over them, brandishing an ugly-looking .45.

"May I ask what you're doing?" he growled.

Mulder held up what he had found in the earth: a piece of raw potato.

"Exhuming your potato," was all he could say.

"May I ask why?" the sheriff asked.

It was a good question. But answering it was not exactly easy.

Scully made the first try. "Sheriff, we know that many serial killers are fascinated by police work. Some even hold positions on their local force. So it is a normal part of our investigation to—"

"Dig up potatoes?" the sheriff asked.

Mulder tried a different approach. "Sheriff, we found out you used to be a dog-faced boy."

He handed the pamphlet to the sheriff and waited for the man's reaction.

Sheriff Hamilton stared at the photo.

Then he chuckled.

"Boy, look how skinny I was back then," he said.

"Then it is you," Scully said.

"Oh, sure," Sheriff Hamilton said, still smiling. "I spent the first half of my life as Jim-Jim. Then one morning I noticed a bald spot on the top of my head. I realized I was not only losing my hair, I was losing my career. Pretty soon all the hair went. My body's still pretty hairy, though. That's why I never go the beach."

"But that doesn't quite explain the potato," Scully persisted.

"Well, it's a bit embarrassing," the sheriff said. "I—got some warts on my hand."

"That *still* doesn't explain the potato," said Mulder.

"Don't you know?" asked the sheriff, surprised. "To get rid of warts, you rub a sliced potato on your hands. Then you bury it under a full moon."

"Oh, sure," said Mulder weakly.

"Right," said Scully. "I guess it just slipped my mind."

"Anyway, how is the investigation going?" the sheriff asked.

After a moment of loud silence, he said, "Not too well, huh?"

"Actually, we expect something to happen any time now," Mulder said.

"Whether we want it to or not," added Scully.

Chapter TWELVE

Conundrum heard a low growling.

At first he thought it was his stomach.

His stomach was always growling. It had growled ever since he could remember. Even the yummiest treat—a nice plump live frog, say, or a canful of wiggling worms, or a squawking mother hen with crunchy feathers—could not quiet it for long.

Tonight, though, his stomach was not making the noise.

By the light of the moon, he saw Hiram Nutt's tiny dog looking at him and growling.

Conundrum looked back at the dog—and licked his lips.

For a moment, though, Conundrum tried to hold back the hunger that raged within him.

He tried to remember what Dr. Blockhead had told him about eating between shows. Bad, bad, bad.

He reminded himself that Dr. Blockhead had sent him out tonight on an errand. Important, important, important.

But his stomach had started growling now. Louder and louder. It drowned out every thought but the thought of fur and bones, eyeballs and blood, and a tender curling tail for dessert.

The tiny dog saw the saliva dripping from Conundrum's mouth. The dog stopped growling. Whining, he turned tail and ran.

Grunting eagerly, Conundrum ran after him. He didn't mind the chase. In fact, he liked it. It gave an extra edge to his appetite.

Conundrum was fast. But the tiny dog was a shade faster—and he didn't have far to run. He reached the Big Top Motor Inn's office door and tore through the doggie flap at the bottom.

A moment later, the office door swung open.

Hiram B. Nutt strode outside. He looked with disgust at the tattooed man slobbering on his doormat.

Safely behind Nutt, his little dog yapped defiantly.

"How many times have I told you?" Nutt said. "Commodore is my pet—not your meal. Try that one more time and I'll kick you and Dr. Blockhead out of your trailer."

Conundrum got to his feet, his head bowed in shame. Why, oh why, did he keep doing such things? Why couldn't he listen to the greatest and wisest man in the world, Dr. Blockhead?

Unfortunately, it was not in Conundrum's nature to answer such questions. Even as he groveled before Nutt, he kept sneaking ravenous glances at the dog.

"What are you doing out this time of night, anyway?" Nutt demanded. "I would think even a blockhead would have enough sense to keep you inside."

Conundrum brightened. At last he had a question he could answer.

He reached down to his loincloth. A piece of paper was pinned to it by a pair of Dr. Blockhead's skull pins. He yanked the paper free and handed it to Nutt.

Nutt glanced at it. "Okay," he said. "Now get back to your trailer—before you bite off more than you can chew."

But Conundrum kept standing there, staring at Nutt's hands.

"I know what you want," Nutt said. "I'll bet Dr. Blockhead promised them to you as a reward. Well, I'm not letting you have the pins—just for being so greedy. You'll have to find some other bedtime snack."

Nutt slammed the door in Conundrum's disappointed face. Then he looked down at the check in his hand and shook his head.

"Tell me, Commodore," he said to his dog, "why

are the weirdo tenants the only ones who pay their rent in advance?"

As if in answer, Commodore started growling, eyes fixed on the door.

Nutt sighed. "He's still lurking around, huh? He's the one who should be turned into dogmeat.

"I warn you," Nutt shouted through the door, "I have a licensed gun! And I'm looking for a good reason to use it!"

Commodore was no longer growling. Instead he was barking angrily.

"What the devil?" Nutt muttered. He opened the peephole in the door. But before he could take a good look, something grabbed his ankle.

He looked down. A small hand had come through the doggie door. It started to pull his leg through it.

"Nooooo!" Nutt screamed. Bracing both hands against the door, he managed to break loose.

He landed half stunned on his back.

He lifted his head—and saw something following the hand through the doggie door.

Something that made him scream again.

And again.

And again.

Until his screams died—and there was only the sound of Commodore, whimpering in the night.

☠   ☠   ☠

Scully heard the pounding on her trailer door.

She refused to open her eyes, hoping the noise would go away.

She was so tired. Sleep was so sweet.

Then she heard the voice shouting.

"Wake up! Wake up, please!"

"Okay, okay, I'm coming!" she shouted back.

Yawning, she got out of bed, snapped on the light, put on her robe, and opened the door.

Lanny stood there. His face was pale as death in the light coming out through the doorway.

"Couldn't this wait until morning?" Scully asked, rubbing her eyes.

"Sorry, miss, sorry, sorry," Lanny babbled. Then his voice broke. "But he's dead, he's dead."

"Calm down, Lanny," Scully soothed him. "Now take your time and tell me, who's dead?"

"My best friend in all the world," Lanny said. "Mr. Nutt! I found him. It was—" Lanny could go no further. He could only shake his head in shock.

Scully was wide awake now.

"Wait here while I get dressed," she said. She closed the door and threw on her clothes in two minutes flat. Then she joined Lanny outside the trailer.

"Let's go," she said. "Show me where you found him."

"Maybe I shouldn't," said Lanny. "Maybe you

shouldn't have to see it. Such a horrible sight. Horrible, horrible, horri—" Lanny started to babble again.

"Don't worry about me," Scully said. "I'm used to bad scenes. It's part of my job."

"You've never seen anything like this," said Lanny. "If you had, you'd never want to look at a dead man again."

Chapter THIRTEEN

Scully crouched down by the doggie door. She wanted a close look at the thin streaks of blood on it.

Behind her Sheriff Hamilton said, "Lanny says the door was locked when he got here. He had to use his key to open it. All the windows are shut and locked from the inside. The only way in was through the doggie door. What could get through that, except a dog? Or maybe a cat?"

Then Mulder said, "Scully, come here."

Mulder was kneeling beside Nutt's body. Scully was careful not to step on the trail of blood between the corpse and the door.

"I don't know what kind of person could fit through a doggie door—but look at this." Mulder lifted Nutt's arm to show Scully the palm of his hand.

A pin was stuck deep into it.

A pin topped with a death's-head.

"Remember where we saw this kind of pin?" Mulder asked.

"How could I forget?" said Scully. "If he can pound spikes into himself and get out of straitjackets, who

70

knows what else he can do? Maybe we finally have a break in the case."

"Maybe," agreed Mulder. "Anyway—" A ferocious thumping sound drowned out his words.

Lanny had been standing in the corner, watching the investigation, taking long pulls from his flask. Now he had started pounding the walls with his fists.

"He was my only friend!" he raved. "He was like a brother to me!"

Scully took a step toward him to calm him down, but the sheriff beat her to it.

He grabbed Lanny from behind in a bear hug.

"Hey there, cool it, Lanny boy," he said. "You're gonna hurt yourself."

"So what?" Lanny mumbled.

"So nothing," said the sheriff. "But you might hurt me in the process—so knock it off."

"He gets like this sometimes," the sheriff told Scully and Mulder. "I toss him in the drunk tank till he dries out. Then he's okay—until the next time."

"You take care of Lanny," said Mulder. "We'll pick up Dr. Blockhead—or I should say, Jeffrey Swaim."

"Right," the sheriff said, hauling Lanny away. Lanny didn't fight him. His body had gone slack. Tears were rolling down his face.

Mulder saw that Scully was staring down at the corpse, shaking her head.

"What's the matter?" he asked her. "Spot something I missed?"

"Not really," said Scully. "It's just that I've been having so many strange dreams lately. I almost expect the crimes to be more—" She paused, looking for the right word.

"Freakish?" Mulder suggested.

"Well—yes," she admitted.

Mulder grinned. "You really shouldn't gripe about this case being routine, Scully," he said. "Not when your main suspect is a human blockhead."

"He's probably snug in bed, like any ordinary citizen," Scully said.

"Complain, complain," said Mulder, knocking on Dr. Blockhead's trailer door. "Can't you get used to the idea that these folks are just like everybody else?"

"Come in—the door's open," Dr. Blockhead shouted.

Scully and Mulder entered the trailer.

Dr. Blockhead was in bed.

A bed of nails.

Scully swallowed hard. She took a deep breath, flashed her badge, and began. "Mr. Swaim. We're federal agents. We're here to question you. Please be advised you have the right to—"

"You'll have to wait a moment," Dr. Blockhead said. "As you can see, I'm a little tied up right now."

He held up his hands. Both of them were holding fishing lines. The lines were attached to fishhooks, and the hooks were embedded firmly in his chest.

"Gives you an idea of what a trout must feel like," he said, giving the lines a tug.

"Mr. Swain," Scully began again, then paused. "Doesn't that hurt?"

"It's a variation on an American Indian Sun Dance ritual," he answered. "I suspend myself by these hooks, and the pain becomes so unbearable that I have to leave my body."

"Leave your body?" asked Scully, and traded looks with Mulder. "Where do you go?"

"You don't understand," Dr. Blockhead said. "It's just a way to free my mind. Or, some might say, my soul."

"I hate to interfere with your freedom, Mr. Swaim," Scully said. "But we're taking you into custody. We want to question you about several recent murders."

"I don't answer any questions until I talk to my lawyer," Dr. Blockhead shot back.

"Who's your lawyer?" Mulder asked.

"I represent myself," Dr. Blockhead declared.

That did it for Scully.

With one hand she pulled out a pair of handcuffs.

With the other she yanked Dr. Blockhead off his bed
of nails.

Scully could handcuff a suspect in her sleep. She
whirled Dr. Blockhead around and put the cuffs on
his wrists behind his back.

"What gives you the right to do this?" he snarled.

"Didn't I mention that we're federal agents?" she
said, clicking the cuffs shut.

"And didn't I mention that I'm an escape artist?"
Dr. Blockhead replied.

"Wha—?" Scully looked down at her wrists.

How did the handcuffs get there?

She didn't get a chance to ask the grinning Dr.
Blockhead.

He gave her a vicious shove, and ran out the
door.

She fell against Mulder, who was coming to her
aid.

He stumbled backward, hitting the edge of the
bed of nails.

And went tumbling right onto it.

"Mulder!" gasped Scully.

He lay motionless.

She reached down to pull him up.

But before she could touch him, he was off the
bed and on his feet. He had to slide out of his jacket
to do it, though. That stayed nailed down.

"Nothing like Irish tweed," Mulder said. "The salesman told me it would keep out the rain and the cold. Didn't mention this, though."

"You're all right?" asked Scully, limp with relief.

"This bed is more comfortable than the one in my trailer," Mulder said. "Are you okay?"

Scully grimaced. She held out her cuffed wrists. Mulder had a key and unlocked them.

They went to the open trailer door and looked out into the darkness.

"Blockhead's off and running," said Mulder.

"It was hard enough to collar him in here," Scully said. "Catching up with him outside will be quite a trick. If he can really leave his body, who knows what else he can do?"

At that moment a large figure walked out of the shadows and up to the trailer.

"Look what I caught," said Sheriff Hamilton. He held up the fishing lines in his hand and gave them a tug.

"Ouch!" said Dr. Blockhead.

Chapter FOURTEEN

"This jail will never hold me!" Dr. Blockhead angrily declared.

"We'll see about that," Sheriff Hamilton said. "We're used to handling all kind of prisoners in the Gibsonton jail. You're not the first escape artist to go behind bars here."

The sheriff had Dr. Blockhead firmly by the arm. Mulder and Scully, guns drawn, followed close behind as they entered the jailhouse. The place was small. The cells were just beyond the sheriff's desk.

"That isn't what I mean," Dr. Blockhead said. "I'm mean that I'm innocent. Your case is based on coincidence. It's a bunch of humbug."

"Humbug?" said Scully. "Really? Well, you're the expert."

Dr. Blockhead shrugged. "Actually," he said, "I'll probably thank you in the end. I'll appear on *60 Minutes* as a victim of mistaken identity. Great publicity for my act."

"Speaking of evidence, does this belong to you?" Mulder asked.

"Oh God, somebody removed the twin," said the sheriff. "Tore him right out."

"I don't think so," said Scully. "I think the twin removed himself."

"Scully, that's impossible," said Mulder. "The twin is part of Lanny, like an arm or a leg."

It was strange for Scully to hear Mulder saying something was impossible. It was even stranger hearing herself disagree.

"Look at the facts," she said. "This hole in Lanny is identical to the hole in all the murder victims. Except for one thing. Lanny is alive—and he's not bleeding."

Before Mulder could answer, the sheriff stepped in. "If you're saying that his twin can crawl out of his body and go gallivanting around town—you're as drunk as he is."

"You said yourself that it's what's inside these 'very special people' that counts," Scully said. "I think that inside Lanny there are special organs that allow his twin to leave him and then rejoin him."

"But Scully, how could you even dream that this twin could—" said Mulder. He could go no further. He could only shake his head.

"Mulder, tell me something," Scully said. "Do you think that an investigator could be led toward solving a case by a dream?"

Mulder needed only a moment to think about it. "It's possible to pick up clues without consciously realizing it," he said. "Those clues are stored in the subconscious. In dreams they could surface. Dreams tell us what we don't know that we know."

"Well, it's possible that something like that happened to me," Scully said. "I've been dreaming of Lanny again and again, as if something was telling me to take a closer look at him. I know it sounds weird, but—"

Mulder stopped her. "Don't apologize, Scully. You're doing just fine. In fact, you're putting me to shame."

"Oh, I don't know about that," Scully said.

At that moment there was another groan from Lanny. His eyes were open and blinking dully. Scully wondered how much he had overheard.

"How . . . how could I . . . ?" Lanny mumbled.

"How could you what?" Scully asked, bending over him.

His words were weak and slurred. "How . . . how could I turn him in? Without . . . without turning myself in?"

"Why is he attacking others?" Scully asked.

"I don't . . . don't think he knows he's harming anybody," Lanny said with agonized effort. "He's just looking . . . looking for another brother."

"You in pain, Lanny?" the sheriff asked.

"It hurts . . . hurts not to be wanted," Lanny said. "I've taken . . . taken care of him all our lives. Maybe . . . maybe that's the reason why . . ."

Lanny reached into an inner pocket of his jacket. He pulled out a spare flask hidden there. He started to raise it to his lips.

Scully stopped him before the sheriff could.

"You've had enough, Lanny," she said softly.

"Had enough. . . ," Lanny vaguely agreed, his eyes starting to glaze.

Before he passed out again, Scully asked, "How long can Leonard survive outside your body?"

"Long enough to . . . long enough. . . ," said Lanny, his voice fading.

Scully grasped his shoulder and shook him gently. "Long enough to do what, Lanny?"

"Long enough to find out you can't change the way you were born," said Lanny with sudden emotion. Then his voice slowed. "But he always . . . always comes back. I am his . . . his only brother."

His head fell.

Scully took his wrist. "His pulse—it's weak," she said.

"We need an ambulance," Mulder said.

"I'll call one." Sheriff Hamilton hurried out of the cell.

Meanwhile, Scully pulled a chair over to the window and stood on it to look out through the bars.

At first glance the spaces between the bars had seemed narrow. Now they looked wide open.

She touched a bar. It was wet with blood.

Mulder and Dr. Blockhead had come to stand by the chair.

"I could sue you for false arrest," Dr. Blockhead said with a triumphant smile. "But a man of my spiritual development would not stoop to an act of such crass greed."

Then he asked in awe, "You mean the twin can do this?" He walked his fingers up the wall. "And that?" He stuck his fingers through the bars.

"It would appear so," Scully said.

"My God," said Dr. Blockhead, "I could sure use him in my act."

"Scully, you're the medical expert," Mulder said. "If you say the twin is able to separate, I believe you. But how mobile can such a thing be?"

"How far can it go?" she said, peering out into the night. "All we know for sure is—far enough to kill."

Chapter FIFTEEN

Scully and Mulder left the cell with their guns drawn.

Sheriff Hamilton looked up from the telephone as they came out.

"The ambulance will be here in a few minutes," he said. "I hope they're in time. Lanny doesn't look so good."

"You wait for them here," Mulder said. "Scully and I will check around outside."

Outside, Mulder and Scully circled the jailhouse until they stood under the window of Lanny's cell.

"Look," Scully said, pointing to traces of blood on the brick. The blood led down from the window to the ground. "The twin must have hands that work like suction cups. They'd have to be close to his body, hidden under the folded sleeves of his jacket. His legs must be short, too. You can't see them under that jacket. But we know how fast they can move."

"You think the hands and feet bleed?" asked Mulder.

"More likely the blood comes from the internal

body parts. The ones that are hooked up with Lanny," said Scully. "Exactly what they are, I can't even guess. It's not the kind of thing I ran into in medical school."

"I think there's something else we can assume about our little friend," said Mulder.

"What?" asked Scully.

"Leonard has teeth," said Mulder. "And they're razor sharp."

Scully nodded. "His mouth could be concealed in the lump of flesh where his head should be. I did notice wrinkles that might be facial features."

"Including eyes," said Mulder. "Leonard seems to know where he wants to go."

"I wish *we* knew where he wanted to go," said Scully.

"He may be telling us," said Mulder. "Look."

Mulder pointed at the sidewalk. In the glare of a streetlight, blood spots gleamed.

They followed the drops around the block and down a dingy street, and then to a large, half-opened door.

"What kind of place is this?" Scully said. It was like nothing she had ever seen before, less a building than a maze of makeshift wooden corridors, spread out over a big vacant lot.

Mulder pushed the door wide open. Inside of the doorway was a switchbox.

"Maybe this will shed some light on it," he said, and pulled the switch.

Outside, Scully's face was bathed in a bright green light.

Above the door a huge neon sign had flashed on. THE TABERNACLE OF TERROR, it proclaimed.

Another neon light showed the faces of a screaming man, a screaming woman, and two screaming children.

"Hepcat's funhouse," Scully said.

"The fun is about to begin," said Mulder. He clicked off the safety catch on his gun. "I hear noises inside. I think we've cornered Leonard. I'll go after him."

"I'll come in from the back and cut off his escape," Scully said. "Be careful in there. We may not be sure how Leonard does it—but we sure know what he can do."

Mulder nodded. He waited until Scully left. Then he started down the long, spooky corridor that stretched before him.

When he reached its end, he saw another corridor branching off it. As he went around the corner, his trigger finger tensed—just in case Leonard was waiting for him.

Nothing came at him. His finger relaxed. Then his whole body stiffened as he saw a pale white shape moving away in the dim light.

Mulder broke into a run. But the shape was already turning another corner.

Mulder increased his speed as he went after it. He raced around the turn, but the ghostlike shape was already out of sight. Mulder didn't know what Leonard used for legs, but the thing could really run.

Mulder sprinted down the empty corridor, then tore around another corner and—

Splat!

Mulder found himself sitting on the floor, shaking his head to clear it.

He had run into a blank wall.

Hepcat must have been laughing his twisted head off, wherever he was.

Meanwhile, Scully had entered the funhouse from the other end. As she went down a corridor, she too had drawn her gun.

She turned a corner and stared into darkness. *A lightbulb must have burned out*, she thought. And there was no Hepcat Helm to replace it. What would this place do without him?

Then she heard a low growl coming from the darkness.

So little Leonard has a voice, she thought. She leveled her gun as she moved toward the menacing sound.

It grew louder.

Her finger tightened on the trigger.

Suddenly a flash of light exploded.

A gigantic head leaped up in front of her. A head with popping eyes and a hideous smile.

Scully recognized its face. It was the face of Hepcat Helm.

Scully lowered her gun as the plastic head dropped into the trapdoor in the floor. The trapdoor closed, and the sound of recorded laughter echoed in the corridor.

"Ha-ha, big joke, Hepcat," Scully muttered as she continued down the corridor.

She reached the door at its end. Holding her gun ready, she opened the door.

She found herself staring into a shiny tubelike tunnel made of mirror-smooth metal. Before she could figure out what it was, she heard a scurrying sound from beyond its far end.

"Leonard! Gottcha!" she said under her breath, running into the tunnel.

"Hey! Whaa—" she gasped, as her feet flew out from under her.

The tube was whirling around and around, like a spinner in a washing machine. Scully was brutally bounced on her back, her sides, her front. Desperately she fought to regain her balance as she hung on to her gun for dear life.

Finally she managed to get onto her hands and

knees. Inch by painful inch, she crawled to the end of the spinning tunnel and out of it.

As she got to her feet, the spinning stopped. The tube stood still, waiting for its next victim.

Scully glared at it as she waited for the spinning in her head to slow.

Then she heard the scurrying sound again, from somewhere farther inside the funhouse.

She looked down the passageway ahead of her.

It looked safe enough, so she started down it.

Her side smashed into a wall. She came off from it and hit the opposite wall. Then the floor fell away from under her feet.

She stood absolutely still.

"I should have known," she said to herself as she took a closer look at the corridor. She saw now that that floor was on a rolling tilt. The walls were adjusted to the tilt so that at first nothing would seem strange. "Very funny, Hepcat, very funny."

She rubbed her shoulder. The bruises from the tube now had new bruises on top of them.

Then she heard the scurrying sound again.

Walking carefully, with one hand on a wall for guidance, she made it to the far end of the corridor.

She breathed more easily when she turned the corner and could stand on a level floor again.

Then her breath caught in her throat.

She saw what she'd been looking for. A milky shape close to the floor.

But it was coming at her faster than she had thought possible.

She had just enough time to aim her gun and fire. Once. And again. And again.

Thank God, at this range, she couldn't miss.

Except that the shape still kept coming as one bullet after another splintered one mirror after another.

Automatically Scully's brain formed the words *Funhouse . . . hall of mirrors*.

But this was no fun. No fun at all.

Pale blobs were coming at her from everywhere. She emptied her gun hopelessly as mirror after mirror shattered into showering glass—and one blob that was left kept coming for her like a living buzz saw.

She braced herself.

Then the blob stopped moving.

Maybe it was hit. Maybe it was tired. Maybe it was as confused as she was.

It didn't matter. At least Scully had a fighting chance against it now. If she couldn't use her empty gun to shoot it, she could use the barrel as a club.

She ran toward it, her gun held high. Savagely she brought the barrel down.

Another mirror smashed, and Scully recoiled in shock.

Then her mouth opened in a silent scream as hands grabbed her shoulders from behind.

Chapter SIXTEEN

"Scully, you all right?" Mulder asked. "I heard shots."

Scully waited a moment for her heart to leave her throat.

"Mulder," she snapped, "didn't anyone ever tell you not to sneak up on people?"

"Sorry, Scully," he said. "Blame the FBI academy. I used to have such good manners before I joined up."

Then they heard a noise from the back entrance of the funhouse.

"It got past me," Scully said. "It's out there and on the loose."

Mulder raced after the sound with Scully right behind him.

Outside, though, they had to stop.

They heard nothing but the silence of the moonlit night.

Mulder put his finger to his ear, then to his lips. He pointed to a nearby cluster of bushes.

Scully nodded. She too had heard rustling in the foliage. She slipped fresh bullets into her weapon as they tiptoed toward it.

But they weren't quiet enough.

A small shape tore out of the bushes at them.

They both raised their guns to fire.

Then both of them froze.

What was coming at them wasn't a pale blob of death.

It was a tiny black bundle of fury, barking in fierce rage.

"Nutt's dog," said Scully as her trigger finger relaxed. "What's he doing here?"

"Trying to tell us something, I think," said Mulder, lowering his gun.

"But what?" said Scully.

Still barking, Commodore stopped before them. He stared up at them. When they made no move, he turned and ran away.

After a few feet, he stopped and looked at them again.

"Hey, boy, what's up?" Mulder said.

Yapping still more loudly, the dog ran back to them. He gave them another pleading look. Then he turned, ran away, stopped, and looked back at them once more.

"Okay, boy," Mulder said. "We get the idea. We'll follow you."

As soon as Mulder and Scully moved toward Commodore, he started running down the street full out. Feet pounding, the agents followed. The dog slowed only when they dropped too far behind. Every time they closed the gap, he speeded up again.

"He's heading for the trailer park," said Mulder.

"He knows who killed his master," Scully gasped. "Spotted him there again. Wants us to catch him. Must have a strain of pointer in him."

"Man's best friend," said Mulder.

"Leonard's worst enemy," Scully said.

When they reached the trailer park, Commodore could not hold himself back.

He ran out of sight among the trailers.

They heard his angry barking from the shadows.

Then, abruptly, the barking stopped.

"I think he's found Leonard," said Mulder.

"Or vice versa," said Scully.

"We'll have to find out," said Mulder, heading toward the shadows.

"I'm not sure I want to," said Scully as she followed.

A minute later all she could say was, "Ughh. Poor thing."

"Leonard must be getting desperate," said Mulder.

"We have to stop him," Scully said, flipping off the safety catch on her gun.

"I wish those clouds would go away," said Mulder. "We need all the light we can get."

Fast-moving black clouds were passing over the face of the moon, making the night dark one moment, bright the next, as if someone were playing with a dimmer switch.

Suddenly Mulder was off and running after a small shape moving between two trailers.

He came to a sharp stop when he reached it.

He took a step backward as a three-foot-tall woman looked up at him and said, "Looking for something, big boy?"

A trailer door opened, and a three-foot-tall man said, "Mabel, you get in here this moment."

After she obeyed, the man said to Mulder, "And as for you, mister—"

He raised a shotgun bigger than he was.

"Look, just a little mistake," Mulder said. He wondered too late if *little* was the best word to use.

"I catch you with my wife again, it's the last mistake you ever make," the man said, and slammed his door.

When Mulder rejoined Scully, she said, "Mulder, don't you wish you had something you could handle better—like little green men from Mars?"

"Right now I feel like I'm *on* Mars," Mulder said.

"I've felt like that ever since we came here," said

Scully. "Gibsonton, home of humbug. Where all boxes are empty, doors turn into blank walls, and everything is as phony as the Feejee Mermaid."

"Everything except death," said Mulder.

They started moving through the trailer park again.

The moon dimmed and the air seemed to chill. Then the moon came out again.

Scully stopped and stared.

"Let's hope that's not what I think it is," she said.

A man lay on his back on the ground beside a trailer.

His hands were clutched over his stomach.

And he was lying still as death.

"That's Blockhead's trailer," Mulder said as he and Scully ran toward it.

"Yeah," said Scully. "Looks like the doctor ran into something sharper than a nail."

"Something he couldn't escape," Mulder said. "I just hope he managed to leave his body first."

Chapter SEVENTEEN

Before Mulder and Scully could reach the body, a light from the trailer came on.

The trailer door swung open.

"What's this—a night raid?" demanded Dr. Blockhead from the doorway. "You Feds better have a warrant—or I'll see you in court."

Scully and Mulder stared at him—then turned toward the body.

Its tattoos were clear in the light from the trailer.

Then Conundrum groaned.

"He's still alive!" said Scully.

By now Dr. Blockhead had joined them.

"What happened to him?" he asked.

"Brace yourself," said Scully as she knelt by Conundrum.

The geek continued to groan as she gently removed his hands from his stomach.

"There's no wound," she said, examining the tattooed skin closely. "There is a bruise, though, and the stomach looks swollen."

"Leonard must have heard us coming," said

Mulder. "Must have run off before he did any real damage."

"If only we knew which way he went," said Scully.

Mulder had an idea. He squatted beside Conundrum. "The thing that attacked you—can you point your finger in the direction he ran in?"

But Conundrum just kept groaning and rubbing his stomach.

"Leonard must have hit him hard," Scully said. "That bruise is black and blue."

"Come on, I'll put some ice on your poor tummy," Dr. Blockhead said to his partner. He helped Conundrum to his feet and led him into the trailer.

Clouds covered the moon again, and once more Scully and Mulder were left standing in the dark.

"We've lost the trail," Scully said.

"Leonard could be anywhere," Mulder echoed.

"We have to do *some*thing," said Scully.

"I agree," said Mulder. "But I don't know what. Except wait here until we hear the next scream."

What they heard next, though, was the sound of a car.

Then they saw headlights. The car stopped, and Sheriff Hamilton got out.

"I was hoping to find you here," he said. "Somebody in town spotted you running in this direction."

"How's Lanny?" Scully asked.

The sheriff shook his head. "Lanny is dead," he said grimly.

"Killed by his own twin," said Mulder. "I guess Leonard tore loose one time too many."

Again the sheriff shook his head. "That wasn't the cause of death. The doc says that Lanny's liver gave out. Too much booze for too long a time."

"That probably explains it," Mulder said.

"Explains what?" the sheriff asked.

"Why the murders have become so much more frequent in the past year—and especially the past few days," Mulder said. "Leonard must have felt Lanny getting sicker and sicker. He must have realized he would die too, unless he found a new person to latch on to."

"That's it," said Scully, remembering the story she had been told of the death of the Original Siamese Twins. "Imagine what it must feel like when the person you're attached to dies. It has to be horrible. I mean, Leonard is human, after all. Maybe when I first got here, I wouldn't have said so. But I see things differently now."

"Human or not, we have to catch him," Mulder said. "He must be desperate. He'll attack anything that moves."

He turned to the sheriff. "Can you help with the

search? And do you have any deputies?"

"So you really think the twin is the killer?" said the sheriff. "I mean, originally you thought it was the Feejee Mermaid."

"This isn't humbug," Mulder said, a touch of anger in his voice.

The sheriff shrugged. "Okay. You're the FBI man. Tell you what. I don't have any deputies, but I do have a lot of friends in town. Special friends."

"Wake them up," Mulder said.

"Yeah," said Scully. "Maybe it takes a 'very special person' to catch one."

By dawn the search was over.

The giant, the midgets, the strongman, the fat woman, the thin man, the three-legged man, the human octopus, a squad of acrobats, and a crew of clowns had gone over every inch of the trailer park.

They had found nothing.

The sheriff broke the news to Scully and Mulder as they stood watching the sun come up. They had been searching all night themselves.

"You're sure it was the twin you saw running around here?" the sheriff asked Scully. "I mean, maybe it was the Feejee Mermaid and she's jumped into the river and started swimming back to Feejee." He smirked, delighted with his own wit.

"Look, Sheriff, there *was* a twin," Scully said, annoyed.

"Relax, Scully," Mulder said. "Now you know what I feel like a lot of the time."

The sheriff turned serious. "You better be sure it was the twin," he said, "if you're letting our friend there get away."

A battered Volkswagen bug was parked next to Dr. Blockhead's trailer. And the doctor was loading it up with his possessions.

Scully, Mulder, and the sheriff walked over to him.

Dr. Blockhead gave them a quick look, and kept on packing. Conundrum was already in the front seat.

"Thinking of taking off?" Scully asked him.

"Wouldn't you be—with that thing still on the loose?" said Dr. Blockhead as he crammed his straitjacket into the last bit of trunk space.

"Leonard is probably dead by now," Scully told him. "He can't have lived this long outside a living body. And his brother is dead."

"I guess it's true what they say—you can't go home again," said Dr. Blockhead.

"I plan to do an autopsy on Lanny," Scully said. "I'm sure I've never seen anything like his insides."

"And you'll never see anything like them again," Dr. Blockhead told her.

"What do you mean?" Scully asked.

Dr. Blockhead's mocking face was solemn for once. "Modern science is wiping out deviant strains of the human form," he said. "In the twenty-first century, genetic engineering will do more than merely eliminate Siamese twins and alligator-skinned people. It will make it hard to find a person with even a slight overbite or a large nose. I can see that future and it makes me shudder. The future looks like—*him.*"

Dr. Blockhead pointed at Mulder.

"Imagine going through your whole life looking like that," said Dr. Blockhead.

Mulder shrugged. "It's a tough job—but someone has to do it."

"That's the reason why self-made freaks like me and Conundrum have to go out and remind people," Dr. Blockhead said.

"Remind them of what?" asked Scully.

"Remind them that Nature hates everything to be normal," Dr. Blockhead said. "It can't go very long without creating something freakish. And do you know why?"

"No," said Scully. "Why?"

"I don't know either," Dr. Blockhead said. "It's a mystery. Maybe some mysteries were never meant to be solved."

"Yeah, like where the twin went," said Sheriff Hamilton.

"I'll leave you with that little puzzle," said Dr. Blockhead as he got behind the steering wheel. "Conundrum and I are off to Baltimore. We open on Tuesday."

Mulder peered into the car.

"Anything the matter with Conundrum there?" he asked Dr. Blockhead. "He looks pretty pale."

"I don't know what his problem is," said Dr. Blockhead. "He kept tossing and turning all night. I couldn't get a wink of sleep. Maybe it's this Florida heat."

"I hope it's nothing serious," said Scully.

She went to Conundrum's side of the car. She leaned in through the open window for a closer look.

Conundrum turned his head so that they were face-to-face.

Conundrum belched.

"Must be something I ate last night," he said.

Scully stood with Mulder and the sheriff watching the Volkswagen drive off.

When it was out of sight, she turned to the others. "I think I'll skip breakfast this morning," she said. "Somehow I've lost my appetite."

LES MARTIN has written dozens of books for young readers, including RAIDERS OF THE LOST ARK and INDIANA JONES AND THE TEMPLE OF DOOM movie storybooks, and many Young Indiana Jones middle-grade novels. He has also adapted many classic works of fiction for young readers including THE LAST OF THE MOHICANS, EDGAR ALLAN POE'S TALES OF TERROR, and THE VAMPIRE. Mr. Martin is a resident of New York City.